MACMILLAN READERS
INTERMEDIATE LEVEL

ELIZABETH VON ARNIM

The Enchanted April

Retold by Margaret Tarner

D0921174

MACMILLAN

Founding Editor: John Milne

The Macmillan Readers provide a choice of enjoyable reading materials for learners of English. The series is published at six levels – Starter, Beginner, Elementary, Pre-intermediate, Intermediate and Upper.

Level control
Information, structure and vocabulary are controlled to suit the students' ability at each level.

The number of words at each level:

Starter	about 300 basic words
Beginner	about 600 basic words
Elementary	about 1100 basic words
Pre-intermediate	about 1400 basic words
Intermediate	about 1600 basic words
Upper	about 2200 basic words

Vocabulary
Some difficult words and phrases in this book are important for understanding the story. Some of these words are explained in the story and some are shown in the pictures. From Pre-intermediate level upwards, words are marked with a number like this: ...³. These words are explained in the Glossary at the end of the book.

Contents

A Note About This Story

This story takes place in England and Italy in 1921. At this time, when people travelled abroad, they went by ferry across the English Channel and then by train. It took about three days to travel from England to the Mediterranean coast.

Telephones were not used very much at this time. Messages were sent by letter or telegram.

The ladies in this story go to stay in a beautiful, medieval Italian castle by the sea. They rent the castle, San Salvatore, for the month of April. This means that they paid the owner of the castle some money to stay there. This money was for the servants and the rooms in the castle. The ladies had to buy their own food and pay for their ferry and train tickets.

The ladies find that the gardens of San Salvatore are very beautiful. In April, many beautiful flowers and trees bloom in Italy. Soon, Mrs Wilkins, Mrs Arbuthnot, Mrs Fisher and Lady Caroline believe that San Salvatore is a magic and enchanted place. Everyone will find love and happiness in this beautiful place.

The People in This Story

Lottie Wilkins
is a young woman. She is
married to Mellersh
Wilkins, but she is
unhappy.

Rose Arbuthnot
is a young woman.
She is married to
Frederick Arbuthnot.
She is not happy.

Mrs Fisher is an old
woman. Her husband is
dead and she has a lame
leg. She has to use a stick
to help her walk.

Lady Caroline Dester
is a rich and beautiful
young woman. She has left
London to get away from
the many young men who
want to marry her.

Mr Briggs is a young Englishman. He is the owner of San Salvatore.

Mellersh Wilkins is Lottie Wilkins' husband. He is a solicitor in London.

Frederick Arbuthnot is Rose Arbuthnot's husband. He is a writer. The Arbuthnots live in London.

These are the servants at San Salvatore. **Francesca** is the maid. **Beppo** looks after the house and the horses. **Constanza** is the cook. **Domenico** is the gardener.

1

The Advertisement

It was a cold afternoon in February. The streets of London were wet and dirty.

Mrs Wilkins was standing at the window of her club[1]. Mrs Lottie Wilkins was tall and thin. Her clothes were dull and old-fashioned[2]. Mrs Wilkins looked down at the crowded street. It was raining again. It was February in London!

Mrs Wilkins' club was not very comfortable, but it was cheap. So Mrs Wilkins sometimes ate lunch there. When she was in the club, she forgot her husband. She forgot her dull life with him in Hampstead[3].

Mrs Wilkins did not want to go home this afternoon. She turned away from the window and sat down at a long table. The table was covered with newspapers. Mrs Wilkins picked up *The Times*.

Mrs Wilkins looked at the advertisements on the front page. Her eyes stopped at the words "To Let[4]".

To Lovers of Sunshine and Flowers

TO LET

for the month of April,
a small Italian castle near the sea

Write to 'Z', Box 100, *The Times*

April in Italy! Sunshine and flowers! Lottie Wilkins sighed[5]. She had £90 in the bank. She had saved the money, penny by penny. But should she spend it on a holiday?

Mrs Wilkins put down the newspaper and went back to the window.

Mrs Wilkins had been married for two years. She had not spent a day away from her husband.

Her husband, Mellersh Wilkins, was a successful solicitor[6]. But it was not easy to live with him. Often, Lottie Wilkins made him angry. Sometimes she forgot things, then Mellersh Wilkins became very angry indeed.

Mrs Wilkins looked at her watch. She had to go and buy some fish for dinner. She turned to leave.

A sweet-faced young woman was reading *The Times* now. Her name was Mrs Rose Arbuthnot. Mrs Arbuthnot and her husband also lived in Hampstead. Mrs Wilkins had seen her there.

As Mrs Wilkins reached the table, Mrs Arbuthnot looked up. She smiled. Then, shy, pale Lottie Wilkins did a very surprising thing. She sat down opposite Rose Arbuthnot and spoke quickly.

'Did you see the advertisement?' Mrs Wilkins asked. 'The one about the castle? The castle in Italy? Did you read it? I'm sure you did!'

'Why, yes, I did,' Mrs Arbuthnot answered slowly.

'I would love to go to Italy, wouldn't you?' Mrs Wilkins said. Her big, grey eyes were very excited.

'Yes, of course I would,' Mrs Arbuthnot answered. 'But it's impossible, I'm afraid.'

'Oh, no!' Mrs Wilkins said. 'If you want something strongly enough you sometimes get it!'

Mrs Wilkins leant across the table.

'Why don't we try?' she whispered. 'Let's rent the castle together!'

'But we don't know each other . . .' Mrs Arbuthnot began.

'It doesn't matter,' Mrs Wilkins said. 'We'll soon be friends. Everyone needs a holiday – even from a husband.

'Perhaps especially from a husband,' Mrs Wilkins added sadly.

Rose Arbuthnot thought of her own husband. She had married Frederick Arbuthnot when she was twenty. They loved each other then. But things had changed.

Frederick Arbuthnot was now a successful author. He wrote clever, amusing books. They were stories about bad, but beautiful women.

Mr Arbuthnot's books were very popular, but Mrs Arbuthnot did not read them.

Mrs Arbuthnot spent her time helping poor people. There were often days when Mr and Mrs Arbuthnot did not see each other. Mrs Arbuthnot's sweet, round face always looked sad.

'I couldn't possibly leave . . .' Mrs Arbuthnot began.

'I'm sure you could!' said Mrs Wilkins. 'I can see us there. I can see us in that lovely garden. Think of it – April in Italy. We'll be so happy there. Why don't we write and find out more?'

'Yes, perhaps I will write,' Mrs Arbuthnot answered slowly. 'I could find out about the rent . . .'

Mrs Arbuthnot stood up. She walked slowly to the writing desk and sat down. She wrote a short letter to 'Z', Box 100.

The two young women left the club in silence. Outside, they said goodbye. Mrs Arbuthnot promised to post the letter on her way home.

'Why don't we try? Let's rent the castle together!'

Mrs Wilkins went to buy the fish for dinner. And Mrs Arbuthnot went back to her lonely house.

2

Making Plans for a Holiday

The owner of the castle in Italy was a young Englishman. His name was Thomas Briggs. He answered Mrs Arbuthnot's letter at once.

The castle had beds for eight people. The rent was £60 for the month. Half of this rent must be paid in advance.

£60! £60 for one month! It was too much. Far too much. Mrs Arbuthnot and Mrs Wilkins could not believe it.

Mrs Wilkins had £90. Could she spend most of it on a holiday? No. Her husband, Mellersh Wilkins, would not allow[7] it.

Mrs Arbuthnot did not tell her husband about the castle. She went to her bank. She took out £60. Then she went with the money to Mr Briggs' house.

Thomas Briggs liked pretty women. He liked Mrs Arbuthnot's dark hair and eyes.

'I am sure you'll be happy at the castle,' he said. 'It's called San Salvatore. It's a beautiful place. You will love it there.'

So Mrs Arbuthnot gave him the £60. Thomas Briggs gave her a receipt[8].

'Now I'm richer,' he said, 'and you're happier. I've got the money and you've got the castle. San Salvatore is beautiful in April. The gardens are full of flowers. You will be another flower in the garden.'

But Mrs Wilkins still had the problem of money. She had to pay half of the rent. Also she had to pay her fare to Italy and she had to pay for food. She could not ask her husband for money. He liked her to save money, not spend it.

So Mrs Arbuthnot and Mrs Wilkins put another advertisement in *The Times*. They wanted two other women to go with them to San Salvatore. They would all share the expenses[9].

Two people answered the advertisement. One was a young woman. Her name was Lady Caroline Dester. Her family was one of the oldest and richest in England.

But Lady Caroline was unhappy and bored[10]. She wanted a holiday. She loved Italy, but she hated hotels. So she was very pleased when she read the advertisement about San Salvatore.

Mrs Arbuthnot and Mrs Wilkins liked Lady Caroline. They invited her to stay at the castle with them.

The second answer to the advertisement was from an old lady. Mrs Arbuthnot and Mrs Wilkins went to her house. Her name was Mrs Fisher. Mrs Fisher was a widow. She was lame and had to use a stick when walking. But she said that she would be no trouble. She just wanted to sit in the sun and remember the past. Mrs Fisher also said that she wanted references[11].

'Why do you want references?' Mrs Wilkins asked in surprise. 'Surely they are not necessary.'

Mrs Arbuthnot stood up. She spoke coldly and clearly.

'References are not necessary,' she said. 'I don't think you

'I don't think you will be happy with us.'

will be happy with us.'

Mrs Fisher thought quickly. She liked getting her own way[12]. She wanted to go to San Salvatore. When she was there, she would give the orders.

'Very well,' Mrs Fisher replied. 'No references. I shall see you at San Salvatore in April.'

Mrs Arbuthnot and Mrs Wilkins left Mrs Fisher's dark house. They got on the bus to go back to their homes. They did not speak for a long time.

'I don't like Mrs Fisher,' said Mrs Wilkins. 'I wish she wasn't coming with us.'

'I think Mrs Fisher is a lonely old woman,' Mrs Arbuthnot replied. 'San Salvatore will be good for her.'

'You are right,' Mrs Wilkins said. 'Mrs Fisher needs San Salvatore too. Mrs Fisher will change at San Salvatore. I'm sure she will.'

———

Mrs Arbuthnot and Mrs Wilkins decided to travel to Italy together. They planned to reach San Salvatore on 1st April. Lady Caroline and Mrs Fisher were arriving on 2nd April. By then, everything would be ready for them at the castle.

The weather in March was cold and wet.

As the days went by, Mrs Arbuthnot became more and more worried. Mrs Arbuthnot was an unhappy woman. She was not used to enjoying herself. She was afraid of change. Now she was planning a month's holiday in Italy. A whole month of pleasure!

When Mrs Arbuthnot told her husband, he looked pleased. He gave her a cheque for £100. Mrs Arbuthnot gave the money to the poor. She felt more unhappy than ever.

Mrs Wilkins was worried too. She did not tell Mellersh Wilkins about her plan to go to Italy. But she gave him special meals every evening. Mrs Wilkins was a good cook. Mellersh was very pleased with her.

On the third Sunday of March, Mrs Wilkins cooked a delicious lunch. After lunch, Mellersh felt pleased and happy.

'I think I shall take you to Italy next month,' he said.

Mrs Wilkins was horrified[13]. She was never happy when she went on holiday with Mellersh. Mrs Wilkins did not know what to say.

Mellersh Wilkins was surprised when Mrs Wilkins did not say anything. Perhaps she had not heard him. So, more loudly, he repeated, 'I think I'll take you to Italy. In April. Didn't you hear what I said?'

'Yes, yes,' Mrs Wilkins said quickly. 'I was going to tell you. I've been invited to Italy – to stay with a friend there. In her house, in April.'

That was a terrible afternoon for Lottie Wilkins.

At first, Mellersh did not believe her. He wanted to know about Rose Arbuthnot. He wanted to know who Rose Arbuthnot was and where she came from. He said his wife could go on holiday. But he was unhappy. The rest of March was like a terrible dream. But Mrs Wilkins had made her plans. She was going to go to Italy with Mrs Arbuthnot.

Mrs Arbuthnot and Mrs Wilkins left London on the morning of 30th March. They were both tired and worried. They did not feel that they were going on holiday.

'We should be feeling happy,' Mrs Wilkins said sadly, as

they got on the train. 'But we are not feeling happy. It's our own fault. We are to blame. We have done too much for our husbands. We have been too good to them.'

Mrs Arbuthnot did not answer. Her husband, Frederick, had been out when she left. He knew his wife was going to Italy for a month. He was not worried that his wife was going on holiday without him. She did not leave her address.

The 30th of March was wet and windy. The sea-crossing between England and France was terrible. The sea was rough and both women were very seasick.

After they landed in France, they began to feel better. They went by train to Paris. From there, they took another train to Italy.

By the afternoon of the next day, the two women had forgotten about Mellersh, Frederick and London.

3

The Journey to Italy

It was cloudy in Italy. Mrs Arbuthnot and Mrs Wilkins thought it was going to be bright and sunny. But the clouds did not matter. The two young women were in Italy and they were feeling very excited.

The hours in the train passed quickly. It began to rain. But they were in Italy. The sun would soon be shining!

Their train arrived at Mezzago four hours late. It was nearly midnight when they got off the train. The two women got down from the train slowly. They felt very stiff and tired. It was dark. The rain was falling heavily. They stood there with their luggage. What was going to happen now?

Suddenly, a young man came out of the darkness. Speaking Italian, he told them his name was Beppo. Still talking loudly, he picked up their cases.

Mrs Arbuthnot and Mrs Wilkins did not know any Italian. But they thought they heard the name "San Salvatore". So they hurried after the young man – and their cases.

A horse-cab[14] was standing by the side of the road. The horse was asleep. The two women climbed into the cab. The horse woke up and began to move.

Beppo ran after the cab and stopped the horse. In Italian, Beppo explained that he was in charge. They would all reach San Salvatore safely.

Beppo thought the English ladies looked pale and tired. So he decided to make them happy. As he drove along, Beppo talked about the beauty of San Salvatore.

'San Salvatore,' Mrs Arbuthnot and Mrs Wilkins said again and again in frightened voices.

'Si, si, San Salvatore!' Beppo cried. And he drove faster and faster along the winding[15] road.

On their left, was a low wall. On their right, were high, black rocks. They could hear the sound of the sea.

'We don't know where he's taking us,' Mrs Arbuthnot whispered.

'No, we don't,' Mrs Wilkins agreed.

They were very frightened. It was so late and so dark. The road was so lonely. The rain was falling so heavily.

'I wish we had arrived in the morning,' Mrs Arbuthnot said sadly.

Mrs Wilkins sighed, but she said nothing.

Beppo began talking again. As he spoke, he turned round to smile at Mrs Arbuthnot and Mrs Wilkins.

Mrs Arbuthnot and Mrs Wilkins wished they knew Italian. Why hadn't they learnt it? They wanted to say, 'Don't look at us. Look at the road.' But they did not know how to say this. So they waved their arms, trying to tell Beppo to look in front.

Beppo thought they wanted to go faster. He was very happy. He shouted and the horse galloped through the darkness. The next ten minutes were terrible. Mrs Arbuthnot and Mrs Wilkins held tightly to the sides of the cab and to each other.

At last, they reached a steep hill. The horse stopped suddenly. Then it began to walk, as slowly as it could.

Here, at last, were houses.

'Castagneto!' Beppo cried.

The horse stopped. They were in a village street. But everywhere was dark and wet.

Beppo got down from the cab. At the same time, a man and several boys ran up out of the darkness. They pulled the luggage from the cab.

'No, no, San Salvatore!' cried Lottie Wilkins. She held tightly on to her cases.

'Si, si, San Salvatore!' they all shouted, pulling hard.

'This can't be San Salvatore,' Lottie Wilkins said.

'I don't think it is,' Rose Arbuthnot replied. But they both got out of the cab.

Two boys opened umbrellas. They handed them to the two women. The man had a lantern. He started to walk along the street. Mrs Arbuthnot and Mrs Wilkins followed.

On they went, down some steps. Then they went up again,

Beppo shouted and the horse galloped through the darkness.

along a stone path. Mrs Wilkins slipped on the wet ground. The man helped her up, and smiled. Perhaps everything was all right. But where was their luggage?

Now they could hear the sea again.

The man pointed. 'San Salvatore!' he said.

'San Salvatore?' Mrs Arbuthnot and Mrs Wilkins repeated hopefully.

They went on. They were very near the sea now. In front of them was an archway[16] and a heavy iron gate. The man pushed the gate open. They went up more steps.

Then they were on a path. The path went up and up. There were flowers. They could not see the flowers, but they could smell them. The scent was heavy and strong.

They saw a light. Was that the castle, high above them? The flowers were everywhere. The warm rain made their sweet scent smell stronger. Higher and higher they went, through the scented darkness.

'San Salvatore!' the man said happily.

'Si, si,' the women answered. And the man said they spoke Italian very well!

Up and up they went. There were more steps and another archway. They were inside the castle at last. In front of them was an open door and bright lights.

'Ecco!' said the man with the lantern. He was Domenico, the gardener[17] of San Salvatore.

They had arrived. This was San Salvatore. And there was their luggage! All was well.

The two women looked at each other and smiled. It was a wonderful moment. Lottie Wilkins put her arm round Rose's neck and kissed her.

'Dear Lottie,' said Rose Arbuthnot.

'Dear Rose,' said Lottie Wilkins. Her eyes were shining with happiness.

Domenico was delighted. The beautiful English ladies were happy! He began a long, fine speech of welcome.

Rose and Lottie were very, very tired. They did not under–stand what he was saying. But they smiled politely. Domenico went on talking . . .

4

San Salvatore

When Mrs Wilkins woke up the next morning, the room was dark. Her watch had stopped. She did not know what the time was.

Mrs Wilkins was not worried. She was alone in her own little room. The room was hers for the next month – a month of peace and happiness. She lay in bed, smiling to herself.

But now she must get up. What would she see from the window? Was the weather good or bad? Mrs Wilkins had to find out. She jumped out of bed and ran to the window. She opened the shutters[18] and the room was full of light.

She was looking down onto the gardens of San Salvatore. Oh, what beauty! Mrs Wilkins could not believe it. The sun was shining and the sea was flat and calm. The air was full of the scent of flowers. What an enchanted[19] place!

Mrs Wilkins took a deep breath. London was very far away.

Mrs Wilkins thought of her husband going to work in the cold and rain. Poor Mellersh! She had almost forgotten him.

Mrs Wilkins washed and dressed quickly. She put on clean, white clothes. She looked at herself in the mirror. What pretty golden hair I've got, she thought. Why have I never noticed it? Why hasn't my husband noticed it?

Mrs Wilkins laughed and began to plan what she would do that morning. She would find Rose Arbuthnot and say good morning to her. Then, after breakfast, they would get ready to welcome Mrs Fisher and Lady Caroline.

At San Salvatore, the bedrooms were on the top floor. When Mrs Wilkins opened her bedroom door, she was standing in a long hall. There was a big window at one end.

The window was wide open. Through it, Mrs Wilkins could see a tree, covered with beautiful pink flowers.

There were pots of flowers in the hall too. Mrs Wilkins had never seen so many flowers before and she loved them.

Mrs Arbuthnot came out of her bedroom. She saw Mrs Wilkins staring at the open window.

'What's the matter?' Mrs Arbuthnot asked quickly.

'Nothing's wrong. Everything is perfect,' Mrs Wilkins answered. 'I was never so happy in my life.'

Holding hands, they walked to the open window. Below them was a little garden. There was a low wall all around the garden. Sitting on the wall was Lady Caroline!

They were so surprised that they stood there staring down at her.

Lady Caroline was wearing a white dress too. She was very, very pretty, with fair hair and pale skin.

Sitting on the wall was Lady Caroline!

'She shouldn't sit in the sun without a hat. She'll get a headache,' Mrs Wilkins said.

Lady Caroline looked up. Her large grey eyes were very lovely. Smiling beautifully, Lady Caroline stood up and walked towards the window.

'Hallo. I arrived here yesterday morning,' Lady Caroline said.

'Oh dear,' Mrs Arbuthnot said. 'We were going to choose the nicest room for you.'

'I've done that for myself,' Lady Caroline answered.

'And we were going to put flowers in it for you,' Mrs Wilkins added.

'I asked the gardener to do that,' Lady Caroline said.

'But we wanted to do it for you,' Mrs Wilkins said. 'I didn't know you were so pretty,' she added. 'You are lovely, very lovely!'

Lady Caroline smiled sadly. Everyone told her she was beautiful. She was tired of it. That's why she had gone on holiday with strangers. She did not want to be friends with anyone.

'I'm sure you must want your breakfast,' Lady Caroline said. 'I had breakfast in my room. I'll see you later.'

Lady Caroline wanted to speak coldly. But her beautiful voice made her words sound kind. So Mrs Wilkins and Mrs Arbuthnot smiled happily. They turned away from the window.

Francesca, the maid, was standing behind them. Breakfast was ready in the dining-room, she said. As she spoke in Italian, the two women didn't understand her. But they followed Francesca downstairs.

Francesca opened the door of the dining-room. Mrs Fisher was sitting at the table, having breakfast!

'Oh!' Mrs Wilkins and Mrs Arbuthnot exclaimed[20] together.

'How do you do,' Mrs Fisher said. 'I can't get up because I have a lame leg.' She held out her hand.

'We didn't know you were here,' Mrs Arbuthnot said.

'We wanted to be here to welcome you,' Mrs Wilkins added.

Mrs Fisher did not listen to what they said.

'Where will you sit?' she asked. Mrs Fisher was sitting at the head of the table[21]. Mrs Wilkins and Mrs Arbuthnot sat down without speaking.

'Tea or coffee?' Mrs Fisher asked. She rang a small bell for the maid, Francesca. There was silence. Then, Mrs Arbuthnot smiled at Mrs Fisher.

'I hope your room is comfortable,' Mrs Arbuthnot said.

'Quite comfortable, thank you,' Mrs Fisher answered. 'There were two beds in my room, but I had one taken out.'

'That's why I've got two beds in my room!' Mrs Wilkins exclaimed.

'I have two beds in my room as well,' said Mrs Arbuthnot said.

'Your second bed is from Lady Caroline's room,' said Mrs Fisher. 'It seemed silly to have two beds in one room.'

'But now we've got two beds in our rooms!' Mrs Wilkins said. 'Can't we have them taken away too?'

'Beds must go somewhere,' Mrs Fisher said coldly. 'Would you like some more coffee?'

'No, thank you. Would you like some more?' Mrs Arbuthnot asked. She said this because Mrs Fisher was her guest. 'Perhaps you would like an orange,' Mrs Arbuthnot added.

'No. I don't eat fruit at breakfast,' Mrs Fisher said. She stood up.

'Let me help you,' Mrs Arbuthnot said kindly.

'Thank you. I am able to walk without help.' And Mrs Fisher walked to the door, quite quickly.

'Well, I'm going to have an orange,' Mrs Wilkins said. 'Rose, do stay and have one!'

'No, I must see the cook,' Mrs Arbuthnot answered. She followed Mrs Fisher to the door.

'What time would you like lunch, Mrs Fisher?' Mrs Arbuthnot asked politely.

'Lunch is at half past twelve,' Mrs Fisher said.

'At half past twelve. I'll tell the cook,' Mrs Arbuthnot said. 'It will be rather difficult, but I've got an Italian dictionary.'

'The cook knows. Lady Caroline told her,' Mrs Fisher said.

'Oh!' cried Mrs Arbuthnot in surprise.

'Yes, Lady Caroline speaks Italian. I do too,' Mrs Fisher went on. 'But I speak the Italian of Dante, the Italian of the poets[22]. And I can't go into the kitchen, because of my stick.'

'But . . .' Mrs Arbuthnot began.

Mrs Wilkins stopped her.

'Then we've got nothing to do but be happy!' Mrs Wilkins said. 'Rose and I have been good all our lives,' she told Mrs Fisher. 'Now we're going to be happy and have a rest!'

Mrs Fisher left the room without another word.

These young women are going to be a problem. I must be strict with them, the old lady thought to herself. They must do as I tell them.

5

Will the Magic Work?

Mrs Wilkins and Mrs Arbuthnot left the house together. They walked slowly down into the lower garden. There were many gardens at San Salvatore. Each garden had different coloured flowers and a different kind of beauty.

'We found San Salvatore. But Mrs Fisher thinks it belongs to her,' Mrs Arbuthnot said. 'It's silly.'

'It's silly of us to worry about it,' Mrs Wilkins answered. 'We have nothing to do. So there's more time to enjoy the beauty.'

And what beauty there was! What magic!

The two women walked down some stone steps. On either side of the steps there were small blue flowers – as blue as the April sky. Here were trees with purple, sweet-scented flowers.

Lower down, the flowers were bright red and gold. Below the gardens were little orchards[23] of olive trees and fig trees. There were other fruit trees too, with flowers of white and pink.

Beneath the trees, there were little bushes. They had purple flowers and grey leaves. And the grass was full of very small white flowers. Far away, at the bottom of the hill, was the sea.

Mrs Arbuthnot felt happy in the warm sunshine. I wish Frederick was here, she thought. We could see this beauty together. She sighed.

'You mustn't sigh,' Mrs Wilkins said. 'People must be happy here in San Salvatore'

'Mrs Fisher isn't happy.'

'She soon will be. Wait and see,' Mrs Wilkins replied. 'She will change. We will like her soon, I'm sure.'

Mrs Arbuthnot laughed.

Lady Caroline, sitting alone, heard Mrs Arbuthnot laughing. What is she laughing about? Lady Caroline asked herself. I don't want to stay a month with women who laugh all the time!

Mrs Wilkins and Mrs Arbuthnot looked up at Lady Caroline. They waved and smiled. Lady Caroline turned her head away and looked at the mountains.

'Perhaps she is unhappy too,' Mrs Arbuthnot said kindly.

'No matter what is wrong, Lady Caroline will forget about it here,' Mrs Wilkins answered.

The two women left the path. They went down and down until they came to the sea.

A pine tree grew near the water. The two women sat under it, in the shade. There was a beautiful sweet scent from the tree and the plants around it. A soft wind blew the scents into the women's faces.

Very soon, Mrs Wilkins took off her shoes and stockings. She put her feet in the water. After a minute, Mrs Arbuthnot did the same. They were too happy to talk.

Far above them, Lady Caroline lit a cigarette. She began to feel better. It was lovely to be alone!

At that moment, the Italian cook, Constanza, walked up to Lady Caroline. Constanza did not know what food to cook for lunch. Mrs Fisher had not told her anything. So Constanza had come to ask Lady Caroline.

Constanza said that Lady Caroline's mother had not told her what to buy for lunch.

'Mrs Fisher is not my mother. My mother is in London,' Lady Caroline said coldly.

They were too happy to talk.

'How sad!' Constanza exclaimed. 'And the young lady's husband is far away in London too!'

'I have no husband,' Lady Caroline replied angrily.

'How sad!' Constanza said. 'Be hopeful. There is still time . . .'

Lady Caroline stopped Constanza talking. 'For lunch,' she said clearly, 'we will have . . .'

Constanza listened carefully and made some suggestions of her own. The food would be good, but very expensive. Lady Caroline did not know this. She agreed to everything.

'That's enough,' Lady Caroline said at last. 'You'd better go now. Lunch is at half past twelve.

'I have ordered lunch and dinner today,' said Lady Caroline. 'But tomorrow, one of the other ladies will tell you what to cook. Now, do go away. I want to be alone.'

But as soon as Constanza left, Domenico, the gardener, came into the little garden. He began to water the flowers.

Domenico watered and watered. And, as he watered, he talked. In the end, Lady Caroline closed her eyes.

'I have a headache,' she said. 'Please go. I want to sleep. I do not want to be disturbed[24].'

'Si, signorina,' Domenico answered. And he went quietly away.

Lady Caroline sighed. She was twenty-eight years old. In another twenty-eight years, she would be nearly as old as Mrs Fisher.

This thought made Lady Caroline feel very unhappy. She stared sadly at the mountains.

But Mrs Fisher was happy.

There were two sitting-rooms at San Salvatore. One was dark. The other was light and pretty. Mrs Fisher decided to keep the light and pretty room for herself.

The room had a glass door. This door opened onto a little garden. This garden had part of the castle wall around it. There was a terrace[25] where Mrs Fisher could walk easily.

But, there was a problem. The other sitting-room had a door which opened onto this terrace too.

Mrs Fisher thought carefully. Then, she called a servant. Very soon, the shutters were closed across the door of the first sitting-room. A cupboard was pushed in front of the door. The room was now very dark. Domenico was told to put some heavy flower pots in front of the door on the outside.

'Now no one can use the door!' Domenico said in surprise.

Mrs Fisher smiled. She then went back to her own pretty sitting-room. She sat there until the gong[26] sounded for lunch.

Mrs Fisher was the first to arrive in the dining-room. She sat down at the head of the table. The others were late. She was not going to wait for them.

'Serve the food,' Mrs Fisher said.

Francesca held out a big bowl of macaroni. Mrs Fisher took some. But she found macaroni difficult to eat. It was so long and slippery!

No one else had come in to lunch.

'Shall I look for the beautiful young lady?' Francesca asked.

'Lady Caroline knows lunch is at half past twelve. They all know,' Mrs Fisher said angrily. 'Go and sound the gong again.'

What bad manners[27], she thought. This is not a hotel.

Francesca knew where Lady Caroline was. She walked out to her, beating the gong loudly.

Lady Caroline was very angry.

'When I don't go to meals, I don't want to eat,' Lady Caroline said clearly. 'Please don't disturb me again.'

And she closed her eyes.

Francesca went back to Mrs Fisher. She told her that Lady Caroline was ill. By this time, Mrs Wilkins and Mrs Arbuthnot had hurried into the dining-room.

'Lady Caroline is ill. Please go out to her,' Mrs Fisher said. 'I can't go because of my stick.'

And to Francesca she said, 'Please serve me the next course.'

The next course was a delicious omelette[28], full of young, green peas.

Mrs Wilkins and Mrs Arbuthnot hurried quickly out into the garden.

When Lady Caroline heard their footsteps, she closed her eyes tightly.

A gentle hand was placed on her forehead.

'I'm afraid you're not well,' Mrs Arbuthnot whispered.

'I have a headache,' Lady Caroline said quietly.

'I'm sorry. Would you like some tea?'

'No.'

Lady Caroline lay without moving. Her eyes were tightly closed.

'Lady Caroline wants to rest. I think she should be left alone,' Mrs Wilkins said.

The two women went back to the house.

'Lady Caroline has a headache,' Mrs Arbuthnot told Mrs Fisher.

'She hasn't got a headache,' said Mrs Wilkins, with a smile. 'She wants to be left alone.'

The others looked at Mrs Wilkins in surprise.

'She said she had a headache,' Mrs Arbuthnot said.

'She was trying to be polite,' Mrs Wilkins explained. 'Soon, she won't have to try to be polite. She'll be polite and truthful all the time.'

'How do you know?' Mrs Fisher asked angrily. She was ready to eat the next course. She rang the little bell to call Francesca.

'Serve me,' she said.

Francesca offered Mrs Fisher the macaroni again. It was completely cold.

6

Lottie Sends a Letter

Lady Caroline was alone. She opened her eyes and looked around. She liked her little garden. She wanted it for herself.

But everyone could see her there. Lady Caroline got up quietly. Taking her cushions and her chair, she walked over to the far corner of her little garden. She was now completely hidden by high bushes.

Lady Caroline laid her head on the cushions. She put her feet on the low stone wall. She thought no one could see her now and so she lit a cigarette.

But Mrs Fisher found her there.

'I hear you are not well,' Mrs Fisher said, in her deep voice. 'The journey has made you ill. We will get some medicine from the village.'

Lady Caroline opened her eyes and stared at Mrs Fisher.

'I knew you were not asleep,' the old lady said. 'You were holding a cigarette.'

Lady Caroline did not answer. She threw her cigarette over the wall.

'I don't like women smoking,' said Mrs Fisher. 'Now, take my advice and go to bed.'

'I don't want to go to bed,' Lady Caroline answered. 'I want to be quiet and to think.'

'Women's heads weren't made for thinking,' said Mrs Fisher. 'Pretty young women are made to be looked at.'

'I don't like being looked at,' Lady Caroline answered angrily.

'And I don't like modern young women[29],' Mrs Fisher replied.

Mrs Fisher turned and went back into the house. She opened the door of her pretty sitting-room. To Mrs Fisher's surprise, Mrs Arbuthnot and Mrs Wilkins were sitting there. Mrs Wilkins was sitting at the desk. She was using Mrs Fisher's own pen.

'Isn't this a lovely room!' Mrs Arbuthnot said happily. 'We have only just found it.'

'I'm writing to Mellersh,' Mrs Wilkins said, turning round. 'He'll want to know that I've got here safely.'

Mrs Fisher stood and stared. The room was full of light and the scent of flowers. But Mrs Fisher was angry.

'You don't like us being here,' Mrs Wilkins said slowly. She stood up. 'Why?' she asked.

'This is my room,' Mrs Fisher said. 'You are using my writing paper. And that's my pen!'

'I'm very sorry,' Mrs Wilkins said, smiling sweetly.

'But why shouldn't we be here?' Mrs Arbuthnot asked. 'This is a sitting-room!'

'There are two sitting-rooms,' Mrs Fisher replied. 'Why should you sit in mine? I don't want to sit in yours.'

'But why . . .?' Mrs Arbuthnot began again.

'Don't worry,' Mrs Wilkins said. 'Things will change you'll see!'

She turned to Mrs Fisher.

'Soon, you'll want us to come and share your sitting-room,' Mrs Wilkins told her. 'Perhaps you will let me use your pen!'

Mrs Fisher took a deep breath. This young woman must not tell her what to think!

'I'm an old woman,' Mrs Fisher explained loudly. 'I need a room for myself. I can't walk far, because of my stick. So I have to sit. And I want to sit in a quiet room. I told you that, in London.'

'We'll be pleased to give you this room if it makes you happy,' Mrs Wilkins said kindly. 'We'll wait until you invite us here. You soon will,' she added, picking up her letter. She took Mrs Arbuthnot's arm and led her to the door.

'Poor old thing,' said Mrs Wilkins, shutting the door behind them.

'She's a very rude old thing,' said Mrs Arbuthnot. 'That room isn't hers.'

'Let her have the room,' Mrs Wilkins said happily. 'It doesn't matter. I'm going down to the post office now. Do come with me.'

They went down the winding path together.

'This is my room,' Mrs Fisher said. 'You are using my
writing paper. And that's my pen.'

'I've been thinking about my husband, Mellersh,' Mrs Wilkins said. 'I've been unkind to him, very unkind.'

'What!' Mrs Arbuthnot exclaimed in surprise.

'It was wrong of me to come to this beautiful place and leave him in London,' Mrs Wilkins said. 'Mellersh planned to take me to Italy himself. Did I tell you?'

'No,' Mrs Arbuthnot replied.

'So you see how selfish[30] I've been. Mellersh has every reason to feel angry and hurt.'

Mrs Arbuthnot could not believe what she was hearing.

'And, what's more,' Mrs Wilkins went on happily. 'I've told him so. It's all here, in this letter.'

'What – everything?'

'Not about the advertisement and spending my savings,' said Mrs Wilkins. 'I'll tell him that when he comes.'

'When he comes?' Mrs Arbuthnot repeated.

'Yes. I've invited him to come here. I want him to share all this beauty.'

'But . . . will he come?' Mrs Arbuthnot asked.

'Oh, I do hope so,' Mrs Wilkins replied. 'The poor man needs a holiday. And I'm sure he'll come.'

When Mrs Wilkins said 'I'm sure' in that way, what she said came true. Rose Arbuthnot looked worried. She did not know if Mr Wilkins would like San Salvatore when he came.

'I know it's strange,' Mrs Wilkins went on. 'In London, I wanted to get away from Mellersh. But I'm so happy here. That's why I want him here too. People change here. There's magic here at San Salvatore, I'm sure!'

Mrs Arbuthnot said nothing. She wanted to write to Frederick. She wanted her husband to come to San Salvatore.

But she knew what Frederick's answer would be:

37

'Glad you're having a good time. Don't hurry back. Everything's fine here.'

Mrs Arbuthnot's eyes filled with tears.

'I don't want to go down to the village today, Lottie,' Rose Arbuthnot said quietly. 'I have to think.'

'All right,' Lottie said, walking on down the path. 'But don't think too long. Write and invite him at once!'

'Invite who?' cried Rose.

'Your husband!'

7

The Magic of San Salvatore

At dinner that evening, the four women sat down together for the first time.

Lady Caroline was wearing a very pretty pink dress.

'How beautiful you look!' Mrs Wilkins exclaimed.

'You must be very cold,' Mrs Fisher said rudely.

For Lady Caroline's arms were bare and the dress was very thin.

'You mustn't catch cold[31], you know,' Mrs Arbuthnot said kindly.

'I'm quite warm, thank you,' Lady Caroline said. She looked across at Mrs Wilkins and smiled. Mrs Wilkins smiled back.

'I've had the most wonderful day!' Mrs Wilkins began.

*At dinner that evening, the four women sat down together
for the first time.*

Mrs Fisher was not interested in Mrs Wilkins' day. She did not listen to what Mrs Wilkins was saying. She turned and noticed that Lady Caroline's wine glass was empty again.

Mrs Fisher pointed to the empty glass. 'Too much wine is very bad for you,' she said.

Lady Caroline took no notice. She was listening to Mrs Wilkins. Mrs Fisher began to listen too. What was Mrs Wilkins saying? Something about a man? Had Mrs Wilkins invited a man to San Salvatore? Nothing had been said in London about men.

'What is this man's name?' Mrs Fisher asked rudely.

Mrs Wilkins looked at her in surprise.

'Wilkins,' she answered.

'Wilkins? Your name?' Mrs Fisher asked.

'Yes. My name and his.'

'Is he a relation?'

'Yes, he is. He's my husband,' Mrs Wilkins explained with a smile.

Mrs Fisher said nothing. She had thought that Mrs Wilkins and Mrs Arbuthnot were widows[32].

They all went on eating in silence. The food was very good. Constanza, the cook, had planned the meal herself. At the end of the week, she would give the ladies the bill. It would be a large bill. But English people usually paid bills without complaining.

Mrs Wilkins was talking again.

'You see,' she said to Lady Caroline, 'we agreed in London that each of us could have one guest.'

'I don't remember that,' Mrs Fisher said.

'I do,' Lady Caroline said. 'But I thought we all wanted to get away from friends.'

'And from husbands,' said Mrs Arbuthnot.

'And one's family – and too much love,' Lady Caroline added.

'Or too little love,' said Mrs Wilkins quietly.

'Too little love is not so bad,' Lady Caroline said.

'Oh, but it is bad!' Mrs Wilkins answered. 'Too little love is like standing in a winter wind, getting colder and colder. That's what it's like, living with someone who doesn't love you.'

'Doesn't your husband love you?' Lady Caroline asked.

'Mellersh? No. I don't think so.'

Mrs Wilkins went on. 'But I'm so happy here, I want Mellersh to enjoy San Salvatore too.

'There are eight beds, but only four people here,' Mrs Wilkins explained. 'We're being selfish. Eight beds need eight happy people. I've asked my husband to come. I want Rose to ask her husband too.

'You haven't got a husband, Lady Caroline,' Mrs Wilkins went on, 'nor has Mrs Fisher, but why don't you both invite a friend?'

Mrs Arbuthnot's face went red. Why did Lottie talk so much about husbands?

Mrs Fisher said, 'There is only one empty bedroom in this house.'

'Only one?' Mrs Wilkins repeated in surprise. 'But aren't there eight bedrooms?'

'Six,' said Mrs Fisher. 'We have four. Francesca has the fifth. The sixth is empty.'

'What a problem!' Mrs Wilkins said.

'What is?' asked Lady Caroline.

'Where to put Mellersh.'

Lady Caroline stared at Mrs Wilkins.

'Isn't one room enough for him?' she asked.

'Oh, yes. But then no one else can have a visitor,' Mrs Wilkins explained.

'Are you planning to put your husband in the one empty room?' Mrs Fisher said coldly. 'There is only one place for your husband to sleep – in your room.'

Mrs Wilkins did not answer. She wanted Mellersh to come but she was enjoying her freedom[33] at San Salvatore. Was she going to lose that freedom, shut up with Mellersh, night after night?

There was a long silence. Then Mrs Fisher said, 'I have a friend. Her name is Kate Lumley. I may ask her to come and stay with me here.'

Silence.

'We now know where your husband is going to stay,' Lady Caroline said to Mrs Wilkins. 'Unless he can't come.'

'But I'm sure he will come,' Mrs Wilkins said slowly.

———

And so, the quiet days passed. The servants at San Salvatore were disappointed. These English ladies never went anywhere. No one came to tea. And, strangest of all, each lady spent the day alone.

Every day, the sun rose, shone down and set. And nothing seemed to happen at all.

But every visitor to San Salvatore was changed by the place. Mrs Wilkins had been the first to change. Quite soon, Mrs Arbuthnot and Mrs Fisher began to change too. And for the first time in her life, Lady Caroline had time to think about herself.

One morning, Lady Caroline went to her little garden, as usual. She passed the time sleeping and thinking.

When she looked at her watch, it was three o'clock. Lady Caroline lay back more comfortably among her cushions.

Now, I'm going to think, she said to herself.

At half past four, Lady Caroline woke up again. She could hear sounds. Tea was being served in her garden.

Suddenly, Lady Caroline decided she was hungry. She got up slowly and walked towards the table.

Mrs Fisher was pouring the tea. Mrs Arbuthnot was offering Mrs Fisher a cake. Lady Caroline sat down. She took a cake and ate it. It was delicious!

'Where is Lottie Wilkins?' Lady Caroline asked at last. No one knew. Lady Caroline liked Lottie. She wished she was with her.

Lady Caroline took another cake. Where was Lottie Wilkins? The three of them ate and drank without a word.

Mrs Fisher was quiet. She felt very well. She could walk quite easily without her stick now. But she was restless. She was not happy with herself. She was too often alone.

Rose Arbuthnot had been thinking. San Salvatore was very beautiful. But Rose wanted someone to share the beauty with her. Someone she loved.

Rose wanted Frederick. But how could she invite him? If he came here, what would they talk about? Rose knew that her husband was not interested in her. He had not been interested in her for the last ten years.

So the afternoon passed. And then it was time for dinner.

They all sat down and Lottie smiled at Rose.

'Has the letter gone?' Lottie asked.

Rose's face went red.

'What letter?' Lady Caroline asked with interest.

'The letter to her husband. Asking him to come,' Lottie explained.

Mrs Fisher looked up. Another husband!

'Have you posted the letter?' Lottie Wilkins asked again.

'No,' Rose answered.

'Oh, well, tomorrow then,' Lottie said.

Rose wished that Lottie would forget the letter. She would never send it anyway.

'Who is your husband?' asked Mrs Fisher.

'Mr Arbuthnot,' Rose answered sharply. She was tired of questions about her husband.

'I mean,' Mrs Fisher went on, 'what is Mr Arbuthnot?'

Rose's face went very red. 'My husband,' she said.

Mrs Fisher was furious[34].

8

Mr Wilkins Arrives

It was the end of the first week. The blossom[35] fell from the trees. The ground beneath the trees was pink and white. The white lilies grew taller. The rose blossoms came out – red, pink and yellow. Purple and yellow flowers covered the grey rocks. The leaves of the fig trees grew thick.

Lady Caroline and Mrs Wilkins now called each other by their first names, Caroline and Lottie. And Mr Wilkins arrived.

Mr Wilkins came on the early morning train. Lottie Wilkins walked down the path to meet him, singing all the way.

As Caroline was dressing, she heard the sounds of Mr Wilkins' arrival.

'Can I have a bath?' he asked, in a loud, clear voice.

Lady Caroline smiled. Having a bath at San Salvatore was an adventure.

The servants began running about, shouting to each other. They were bringing wood, making a fire to heat the water.

The printed instructions on the bathroom wall were very clear. They repeated the word "danger" several times. But Mr Wilkins didn't understand Italian.

Mr Wilkins was very surprised when Domenico tried to get into the bathroom with him. Domenico tried to explain. If the hot water tap was turned off too soon, the stove would blow up[36].

Mr Wilkins did not know this. He pushed Domenico away and locked the bathroom door. He got into the bath and turned off the tap.

And the stove blew up! No one was hurt, but it made a terrible noise.

Mr Wilkins jumped out of the bath, wrapping a towel around himself. He unlocked the bathroom door and ran out into the hall.

'That damned bath!' cried Mr Wilkins. He was very angry. He was even more angry when he saw Lady Caroline running out of her room. Mr Wilkins knew immediately who Lady Caroline was.

Mr Wilkins had come to San Salvatore because he knew Lady Caroline was there. Her family was very rich and

45

important. Such families often needed good solicitors. Mr Wilkins was a good solicitor. He was always looking for business.

So, when Mellersh Wilkins received Lottie's letter, he sent her a telegram at once. Now, here he was, standing in front of Lady Caroline dripping with water, wearing only a towel. Mr Wilkins felt very silly.

But Lady Caroline had perfect manners.

'How do you do,' she said, and held out her hand.

'How do you do,' Mr Wilkins answered. 'Am I speaking to Lady Caroline Dester? My name is Mellersh Wilkins.'

Lady Caroline nodded and smiled.

'I thought you were Lottie's husband,' she said, with another smile.

By this time, the servants had come running up the stairs. Mrs Fisher came out of her room.

'Let me introduce Mellersh Wilkins,' Lady Caroline said. 'Mr Wilkins, this is Mrs Fisher.'

Mr Wilkins shook hands with Mrs Fisher.

'It is a pleasure to meet a friend of my wife's,' he said politely.

They all met again at dinner. It was a very successful evening. Mr Wilkins liked Mrs Arbuthnot. He thought she was a very pleasant lady. Also, he saw that Mrs Fisher sat at the head of the table! Perhaps Mrs Fisher was rich. Perhaps she needed a solicitor too.

But the next day, Constanza the cook wanted someone to

'How do you do? Am I speaking to Lady Caroline Dester?
My name is Mellersh Wilkins.'

pay the housekeeping bills[37]. Mrs Fisher and Lady Caroline would not listen to her. Constanza looked for Mrs Arbuthnot, but she could not find her anywhere.

At last, Constanza found Lottie and Mellersh Wilkins. She held out several pieces of paper, covered with figures.

'Does this lady want something?' Mr Wilkins asked.

'Money. She wants money,' Lottie said sadly. 'It's the housekeeping bills.'

'But you are Mrs Arbuthnot's guest. You have nothing to do with bills,' Mellersh Wilkins said, with a smile.

'Oh, yes I have,' Lottie answered. She began to explain that she was not a guest at San Salvatore. She was spending her own money. To Lottie's surprise, Mellersh Wilkins was not angry at all. He smiled and told Constanza to go away.

Constanza went back to Mrs Fisher. Constanza knew that the old lady could understand Italian. Constanza told Mrs Fisher that the bills must be paid. If she did not have the money, there would be no food the following week.

Mrs Fisher took the bills and looked at the total. It was very large. Mrs Fisher took Constanza into her sitting-room. Then she checked every bill, slowly and carefully.

Constanza was with Mrs Fisher for half an hour. Mrs Fisher asked questions about everything. Constanza began to cry. Mrs Fisher went on talking. Mrs Fisher spoke to Constanza in her beautiful, poetic Italian.

Constanza would not be given any money until the following week. But the food must be as good as before.

Constanza cried louder. Mrs Fisher sent her away. Then Mrs Fisher went to find Lady Caroline. On the way, Mrs Fisher met Mr Wilkins.

'I'm very angry with Lady Caroline,' Mrs Fisher said. 'She

was to do the housekeeping. But the cook has been doing what she likes!'

'Lady Caroline looking after the housekeeping?' Mr Wilkins exclaimed in surprise. 'But she's a Dester. She doesn't do housekeeping.'

'I don't care who she is,' Mrs Fisher said rudely. 'I have to be careful with my money!'

Mrs Fisher and Mr Wilkins found Lady Caroline in her garden.

'You should have checked the bills,' Mrs Fisher told Lady Caroline. 'What are you doing about next week's bills?'

'Nothing,' answered Lady Caroline, with a smile.

'Nothing?' Mrs Fisher repeated angrily.

'May I make a suggestion?' Mr Wilkins said. 'Give the cook some money every day. Not much money, of course. And her meals must be as good as before.'

'But what about these terrible bills?' Mrs Fisher asked.

'I will pay them,' Lady Caroline said quietly. 'That is my present to San Salvatore.'

There was silence.

'And now, Mrs Fisher,' Mr Wilkins said pleasantly, 'perhaps you will show me the gardens.'

Mrs Fisher was delighted. Mr Wilkins led her away, talking politely. He had noticed that Lady Caroline wanted to rest. The daughter of the Desters must not be disturbed!

9

A Telegram for Rose

When the second week began, everyone was happy. Everyone liked Mr Wilkins and he was very pleased with Lottie. She had made some very useful friends.

Rose Arbuthnot decided to write to Frederick. Mr Wilkins had changed at San Salvatore. Perhaps Frederick Arbuthnot would change too.

Rose sat down several times to write the letter. But every time, she changed her mind and tore it up.

Mrs Fisher was very restless. She was not happy with herself. She could not understand why. The sunshine and flowers of San Salvatore were changing her too. She was beginning to feel young again. It was a very strange feeling. She could not sit still. She walked up and down on the terrace of her little garden.

The golden days of the second week went by. New flowers blossomed with sweeter scents and brighter colours. San Salvatore became more and more beautiful.

On the first day of the third week, Rose made her decision. She wrote to Frederick, asking him to come to San Salvatore. Then she gave the letter to Domenico to post.

Two days went by. Frederick must have my letter by now, Rose thought. Mr Wilkins had replied by telegram. Would Frederick Arbuthnot send a telegram too?

Rose sat alone all morning. She sat under the pine tree near the sea. The hours passed very slowly. Rose stayed away from the house until lunch-time. She hoped and hoped that a telegram would come.

Just before half past twelve, Rose walked slowly back to the house. She walked very slowly, stopping to smell the flowers as she passed.

She reached the house at last. Mr Wilkins was standing in the doorway. He was holding an envelope in his hand.

'A telegram has come for you!' he called.

Rose's heart was filled with joy. She ran up the steps and took the telegram. She opened the envelope with trembling fingers.

'Not bad news, I hope?' Mr Wilkins said. For Rose's face had gone very white.

Rose looked up at Mr Wilkins sadly.

'Bad news? Oh, no. Not at all. I'm going to have a visitor,' Rose said.

She held out the telegram. Mr Wilkins took it and read it aloud.

I'M ON MY WAY TO ROME.
MAY I CALL THIS AFTERNOON?
THOMAS BRIGGS

'Who is Thomas Briggs?' Mr Wilkins asked in surprise.

'Thomas Briggs?' Rose repeated. 'Oh, he's the owner of San Salvatore.'

Mr Wilkins could not understand why Rose looked so sad.

———

Thomas Briggs was on his way to San Salvatore. He wanted

to see Rose Arbuthnot again. He remembered Rose's dark eyes and sweet, round face. He wanted to see Rose at San Salvatore. There was an old painting there which looked exactly like Rose.

All the villagers in Castagneto greeted Thomas Briggs happily.

Very soon, he was walking up the winding path to San Salvatore.

The door was open. Mr Briggs remembered that he was a visitor. He rang the bell.

Francesca came to the door. She held up her hands in surprise. Briggs spoke to her in Italian.

'Please take my card[38] to your mistress,' he said.

'Which mistress? There are four,' Francesca answered.

'Four?' Briggs repeated. 'Then take my card to all of them!' Francesca hurried into the garden. Briggs walked inside and stood in front of the painting that looked like Rose Arbuthnot. Yes, the sweet, round face and dark eyes were exactly the same.

Then, Rose herself came down the stairs.

'How do you do,' Rose asked sadly.

'Please, please stand there,' Thomas Briggs cried. 'Would you mind taking off your hat?'

Very surprised, Rose took off her hat.

'I thought so. Your hair is the same, too. Look!' he said, pointing at the painting.

'Is that why you've come? To see if I look like the painting?' Rose asked, with a smile.

Before Briggs could answer, Francesca came back.

'The Signora Fisher will be pleased to see you,' she said loudly.

'Who is Signora Fisher?' Thomas Briggs asked.

'There are four of us staying here,' Rose explained. 'It was too expensive for my friend and me to come here by ourselves.'

'Oh, I had no idea . . .' Briggs began. He wanted Rose to be his guest. He wanted her to stay as long as she liked.

'I'll take you to Mrs Fisher,' Rose said kindly. 'She's in the top garden.'

'I don't want to see Mrs Fisher,' Briggs said quickly. 'We are going for a walk. I want to be with you.'

'Very well. You can meet Mrs Fisher at tea,' Rose said, with a beautiful smile.

'Do you speak Italian?' Briggs asked.

'No, why?' Rose said.

Briggs turned to Francesca. Speaking in Italian, he gave her a message for Mrs Fisher. He was going for a walk with his old friend, Rose Arbuthnot, until tea-time.

'Now, show me the gardens!' Thomas Briggs said to Rose. Rose Arbuthnot realized that she did not bore Mr Briggs at all!

———

Thomas Briggs and Rose Arbuthnot had a very enjoyable walk. Briggs thought that Rose looked pretty and was intelligent. He spoke to her about his life and what he wanted to do. Rose heard herself saying interesting and amusing things. She wished that Frederick could hear her.

Briggs looked at all the beauty around him. He laughed happily.

'I have no brothers or sisters,' he explained to Rose. 'But

you make me feel part of a family. You and San Salvatore go well together.'

Rose brought Thomas Briggs back to the garden near the house for tea. She was smiling – a happy woman. Mr Wilkins noticed this at once. He welcomed Mr Briggs cheerfully.

Mrs Fisher was very polite. Thomas Briggs thought that she was a lovely old woman. Very soon, Mrs Fisher was calling Briggs 'my dear boy'. She laughed. No one had ever heard Mrs Fisher laugh before.

Yes, Mrs Fisher was happy at last. It was the magic of San Salvatore!

When Lottie came to tea, she understood what had happened. Lottie bent over Mrs Fisher and kissed her.

'Good heavens!' Mrs Fisher exclaimed. She pressed Lottie's hand and smiled at her.

Thomas Briggs told everyone that he was going to Rome in the morning.

'I shall spend the night in the village,' he added.

'No, no, you must stay here,' Lottie said. 'It's your house and there is an empty bedroom.'

'That's right, my dear boy, stay here with us,' Mrs Fisher said.

'Yes, do,' said Rose.

'How kind of you all,' Thomas Briggs said happily. 'I'm so happy to be a guest at San Salvatore. The guest of three such . . .' He stopped.

'Didn't Francesca say there were four ladies here?' he asked.

'That's right. You haven't met Lady Caroline,' Lottie said.

'Good heavens!' Mrs Fisher exclaimed.

'Lady Caroline . . .?' Briggs began. Then he stopped. There, walking towards them, was Lady Caroline herself.

Briggs could not speak. Lady Caroline was the most beautiful woman he had ever seen. Thomas Briggs had fallen deeply in love!

10

Another Visitor At San Salvatore

Lady Caroline knew immediately what had happened. Men were always falling in love with her.

Briggs said a few words and his face went bright red. Lady Caroline turned her head away. Briggs looked at her beautiful face. He fell deeper and deeper in love.

'Where is your luggage, Mr Briggs?' Mrs Fisher asked. 'Can someone bring it for you?'

'Oh, yes, my luggage,' Thomas Briggs repeated. 'I'll send Domenico . . . I'm sorry, I'm a guest here. I'll get it myself.'

'We can easily send Domenico,' Rose said sweetly.

Briggs turned to look at her. Rose was pretty. But Lady Caroline . . . Lady Caroline was the woman of his dreams. She was a perfectly beautiful woman. She had completely enchanted him. Everyone noticed it.

Lady Caroline finished her cigarette and stood up. She wanted to stay in the garden and watch the sun setting over the sea. But if she did, she knew Thomas Briggs would stay with her.

Lady Caroline began to walk towards the house. Thomas Briggs followed her.

'I hope Francesca is taking care of you,' he said. 'Please tell me if there is anything you need.'

'I'm very comfortable, thank you,' Lady Caroline said. They walked on through the hall.

'Where are you going to sit?'

'In my own room,' Lady Caroline answered. She began to walk upstairs.

'Then I won't see you again before dinner?' Briggs asked.

'Dinner is at eight,' Lady Caroline answered.

Mr Briggs sadly watched her go. Then he walked slowly back into the garden.

Lady Caroline sat down in her room and sighed. Another young man had fallen in love with her. Wherever she went in San Salvatore, Thomas Briggs would be there. She wished that Mrs Fisher had invited her friend, Kate Lumley. Then Thomas Briggs would not have had a room to stay in.

Lady Caroline suddenly felt angry. She wanted to be in the garden. She got up and looked out of her window.

Mr Wilkins was talking to Mr Briggs. And Mr Briggs had his back turned towards the house.

Lady Caroline ran downstairs and out into the cool air. She walked quickly down the winding path happy to be away from everyone.

Everything was quiet and cool. A sweet scent came from the flowers. Lady Caroline sat down and took a deep breath. Ah, this was . . .

Suddenly, she heard a noise. Someone was on the path. Had Thomas Briggs found her? No. The footsteps were coming up the path, not down. Lady Caroline turned her head.

A man was standing there – a man Lady Caroline knew. She stared at him in surprise. It was Mr Ferdinand Arundel, the well-known writer of amusing biographies[39]. Lady Caroline had often met him in London.

'You?' Lady Caroline said in surprise. 'Here? How did you . . . ?'

The man took off his hat. He smiled nervously.

'You must forgive me, Lady Caroline,' he said. 'Your mother told me you were here. I was on my way to Rome. I thought I would call and see you.'

'But I came here for a complete rest. I wanted to get away from everyone.'

'Yes, I know. I'm sorry. But I had to see you again.'

Lady Caroline thought quickly. Mr Arundel might keep Thomas Briggs away from her. She decided to be friendly.

'Dinner is at eight,' Lady Caroline said. 'You must come up to the house and dine with us.'

'May I?' Mr Arundel said. 'That is very kind of you. Perhaps I could sit down here for a moment and rest.'

Lady Caroline was lovelier than he remembered. Mr Arundel was happy just to look at her and hear her voice again.

'Your mother said you were staying with strangers,' Mr Arundel said. 'Who are these people?'

'I found them in an advertisement,' Lady Caroline said with a laugh. 'They are all very kind. I like one of them very much.'

'Do tell me about her.'

'Wait until you see her!' Lady Caroline answered. 'Now tell me how my mother is.'

Mr Arundel began talking in his usual lively way. Time passed. It began to get dark.

'Good heavens! It's a quarter to eight!' Lady Caroline cried. 'I'll go up to the house and tell Francesca that we have another guest.'

Lady Caroline ran quickly up the winding path. Mr Arundel, who was quite fat, followed more slowly. Francesca came down the path to meet him. Taking him into the house, she showed him where to wash.

Soon Ferdinand Arundel was in the drawing-room[40]. He stood by the window, looking out at the gardens. The house was very quiet.

Upstairs, Rose Arbuthnot was sitting at her bedroom window. She was thinking about Thomas Briggs. For a short time, he had liked Rose. Now he was completely in love with Lady Caroline. Rose did not mind. Thomas Briggs had made her feel pretty and amusing again.

Rose smiled. Perhaps she was pretty and amusing! How she wished Frederick was here now. Then he would see how different she was. She was tired of their cold, separate lives. Rose wanted to love and be loved again.

It was a few minutes to eight. Rose decided to go out into the gardens before dinner.

On her way outside, Rose passed the door of the drawing-room. The firelight shone through the open door. How pretty the room looked. She stood in the doorway.

There were flowers on the table. The room was full of their scent. Rose went into the room and then stopped. The room was not empty. A man was standing by the window.

Rose stood quite still. Her heart beat faster and faster. It was Frederick. He had come. He had come. He must love her – he must!

Rose tried to speak, but no sound came out. She moved slowly towards the window.

'Frederick,' she whispered.

The man turned quickly.

'Rose!' he exclaimed.

But Rose did not see his look of surprise. Her arms were around his neck.

'I knew you would come. In my heart, I knew you would come,' Rose whispered.

'Frederick,' she whispered.

11

Magic and Moonlight

Ferdinand Arundel was Rose's husband, Frederick.

Frederick was very surprised to see his wife at San Salvatore. But she was not surprised to see him. He could not understand it. And why was Rose, his cold, unhappy wife, kissing him?

Frederick Arbuthnot was not an unkind man. There was only one thing he could do. Kiss Rose! It was the right thing to do and he enjoyed it.

Frederick began to feel young again. And Rose, his Rose, was the girl he had once loved so much. With Rose, he felt comfortable. Rose didn't mind that he was forty and getting fat. Rose was his own dear wife. She loved him and he loved her.

'When did you leave London?' Rose whispered.

'Yesterday morning,' Frederick replied quietly.

'Oh,' said Rose, 'the very minute you got my letter!'

'Yes,' said Frederick. So Rose had sent a letter! Frederick kissed Rose again.

'Dearest, dearest,' he whispered.

'Beloved husband,' Rose replied.

At that moment, Thomas Briggs came into the room. He was looking for Lady Caroline.

'I'm sorry . . .' Briggs began.

'Oh, Mr Briggs. This is my husband,' Rose said happily. 'Frederick, Mr Briggs is the owner of San Salvatore.'

The gong sounded for dinner. A few minutes later, Mrs

Fisher walked into the room. Behind her, came Mr Wilkins. Lottie came in after him.

Rose introduced Frederick to everyone.

'What a delightful place this is!' Frederick said.

'Yes, San Salvatore is an enchanted place,' Lottie Wilkins told him.

'We won't wait any longer for dinner,' Mrs Fisher said. 'Lady Caroline is always late.'

Frederick Arbuthnot went cold. He suddenly remembered. He had come to see Lady Caroline, not his wife. Lady Caroline thought his name was Ferdinand Arundel. She did not know that he was married. What would she say?

They walked into the dining-room and sat down. They began to eat in silence. The food was delicious.

The door opened and Thomas Briggs jumped to his feet as Lady Caroline came in. Frederick Arbuthnot stood up too. What an extremely difficult situation!

Lady Caroline sat down quietly. Lottie leant across the table.

'Caroline, this is Rose's husband, Frederick Arbuthnot,' Lottie said. 'Hasn't he got here quickly?'

Lady Caroline turned to Frederick with a smile. She held out her hand.

'Welcome to San Salvatore, Mr Arbuthnot,' Lady Caroline said politely. 'I am late for dinner on your first evening. I'm so sorry.'

Frederick gave a sigh of relief. Lady Caroline was not going to tell Rose the true story.

That night, there was a full moon. The garden was an enchanted place. In the moonlight, all the flowers looked white. Their scent filled the air.

The three younger women were sitting on the low wall of the little garden. The men were talking in the dining-room. Mrs Fisher was by the fire in the drawing-room.

Rose was looking at the big round moon, shining on the water. Rose was shining too. Shining with happiness.

Lottie whispered, 'It's love, Caroline. It's the magic of love!'

Lady Caroline nodded her head. Love again, she thought. Love was everywhere. She looked up at the stars. We fall in love with beauty, she thought. And love makes us beautiful.

Lottie whispered again.

'Rose's husband looks plain to us, a rather round, red-faced man,' Lottie said. 'But Rose doesn't see that because she loves him.'

Lady Caroline got up and walked away. She sat down in her hidden corner of the garden and thought about love. Love was great and strong. But she felt small and very alone.

The three men came out into the garden. Lady Caroline looked at Thomas Briggs. He was young, handsome and intelligent. Thomas Briggs had fallen in love with her because she was beautiful. But Caroline wanted to tell him what she was like. She knew she was cold and selfish.

Lady Caroline stood up. Frederick saw her and walked over to speak.

'I must thank you,' Frederick whispered. 'Now we will always be friends, won't we?'

Lady Caroline held out her hand. Frederick kissed it and walked away.

'Where is your luggage?' Lady Caroline called after him.

'Oh, I forgot. It's at the station,' Frederick answered.

'I'll send Domenico,' Caroline said. And she went indoors to find him.

When Caroline went back out into the garden, Rose and Frederick were walking away together. Then Caroline saw Thomas Briggs standing alone.

Caroline made a decision. She walked over to the young man and smiled.

'I have so much to thank you for,' she said.

'No, no,' Thomas Briggs cried. 'I must thank you. I am so happy to have you here!'

Caroline shook her head.

'I am the one who has found happiness here,' she said.

Thomas Briggs took a step towards her. He held out his arms; his eyes were full of love. Caroline smiled and moved towards him.

Mr Wilkins saw what was happening.

'I must stop this,' he whispered to Lottie. 'It's the magic of the moonlight. They will not feel the same in the morning.'

Lottie took hold of his arm.

'I want to tell you something, Mellersh,' she said.

'Not now, Lottie,' Mellersh Wilkins replied. 'I must speak to . . .'

But Lottie was leading him away.

'Caroline is all right now,' Lottie said. 'Let's go inside and talk to Mrs Fisher.'

Mrs Fisher was sitting alone. She was looking thoughtfully at the fire. Lottie went up to her and kissed her. Mrs Fisher smiled and held Lottie's hand for a moment.

Lottie put a cushion under Mrs Fisher's feet.

'I have so much to thank you for,' she said.

'Thank you, Lottie dear,' Mrs Fisher said. 'Where are the others?'

'They have all gone walking in the gardens,' Lottie replied.

———

In the last week of the enchanted April, the sweetest and most beautiful flowers came out in San Salvatore. The gardens were full of a new, strong scent. The gardens and trees were covered with pure white flowers.

On the first of May, everyone left San Salvatore. They had all changed and they were all completely happy.

At the bottom of the winding path, they looked back at the beautiful gardens. Then, they closed the gates behind them. The air was full of the scent of flowers.

Points for Understanding

1

1 Describe Mrs Wilkins.
2 What was life like for Mrs Wilkins in Hampstead?
3 Mrs Wilkins saw an advertisement in *The Times*. A castle was 'To Let'.
   (a) Where was the castle?
   (b) How long was it to let?
   (c) In which month was it to let?
4 Why was Mrs Wilkins' husband not easy to live with?
5 Mrs Wilkins spoke suddenly to Mrs Arbuthnot.
   (a) What did Mrs Wilkins suggest?
   (b) Did Mrs Arbuthnot agree?
6 What kind of books did Frederick Arbuthnot write? Did Mrs Arbuthnot enjoy reading them?
7 Why did Mrs Arbuthnot always look sad?
8 Write a letter to 'Z', Box 100 asking about the rent of the castle in Italy.

2

1 The owner of the castle was a young Englishman called Thomas Briggs. He answered Mrs Arbuthnot's letter at once.
   (a) How many beds were there in the castle?
   (b) How much did the castle cost for one month?
   (c) What did Mrs Arbuthnot do?
2 Mrs Wilkins had a problem.
   (a) What was her problem?
   (b) How was the problem solved?
3 What kind of person was Lady Caroline Dester?
4 Why did Mrs Arbuthnot think at first that Mrs Fisher would not be happy with them?
5 Why did Mrs Fisher change her mind about references?
6 When Mrs Arbuthnot told her husband, he gave her a cheque.
   (a) What was the value of the cheque?
   (b) What did Mrs Arbuthnot do with the money?

7 What terrible shock did Mellersh Wilkins give Mrs Wilkins on the third Sunday of March? Why was it a terrible afternoon?
8 How did the two women feel when they left London on 30th March?

3

1 What time was it when the two women arrived at Mezzago? What was the weather like?
2 Why were the two ladies afraid of Beppo?
3 Why did Beppo think the English ladies wanted him to drive faster?
4 How did the ladies know there were flowers on the path around them?
5 Domenico began a long speech of welcome. Why could the ladies not understand one word of it?
6 Who is
   (a) Lottie?
   (b) Rose?
   (c) Why are the first names being used suddenly?

4

1 Mrs Wilkins could not believe it. Why did Mrs Wilkins think she was in an enchanted place?
2 Who had Mrs Wilkins almost forgotten?
3 When had Lady Caroline arrived?
4 Why had Lady Caroline gone on holiday with strangers?
5 Why was Mrs Fisher sitting at the head of the table?
6 Why were Mrs Wilkins and Mrs Arbuthnot upset about the beds in their bedrooms?
7 Who did Mrs Arbuthnot think should be the leader of the holiday? Why? Did Mrs Fisher agree?

5

1 Mrs Arbuthnot was angry with Mrs Fisher.
   (a) Why was Mrs Arbuthnot angry?
   (b) What did Mrs Wilkins think?

2 Describe the garden at San Salvatore.

3 Who did Mrs Arbuthnot wish was at San Salvatore with her?

4 The cook, Constanza, did not understand two things about Lady Caroline. What were the two misunderstandings?

5 The food which Lady Caroline told Constanza to buy for lunch was going to be good. Was it going to be cheap?

6 Mrs Fisher showed that she was a very selfish woman in two ways. What were these two ways? Think about:
   (a) what she did in the sitting-room.
   (b) how she ate her lunch.

7 'Lady Caroline has a headache,' Mrs Arbuthnot told Mrs Fisher.
   (a) Did Mrs Wilkins agree?
   (b) What did Mrs Wilkins say Lady Caroline wanted?
   (c) Was Mrs Fisher pleased?

6

1 Describe the disagreement between Lady Caroline and Mrs Fisher.

2 Why was Mrs Fisher angry with Mrs Arbuthnot and Mrs Wilkins?

3 Mrs Arbuthnot was very angry with Mrs Fisher. What did Mrs Wilkins say to Mrs Arbuthnot?

4 Mrs Wilkins had written a letter.
   (a) Who was the letter addressed to?
   (b) Why did Mrs Wilkins think she had been selfish?
   (c) What had Mrs Wilkins said in the letter?

5 What did Mrs Wilkins say had happened to her in San Salvatore?

6 Does Mrs Arbuthnot think her husband would come to San Salvatore?

7

1 Mrs Fisher was twice rude to Lady Caroline. How was she rude?

2 What agreement did Mrs Wilkins say that they had made in London about guests?

3 How did Mrs Wilkins describe living with someone who does not love you?

4 How many bedrooms were there in the castle? Who slept in the bedrooms?

5 Where did Mrs Wilkins want her husband to sleep? Why did she not want her husband to sleep in her bedroom?

6 Mrs Fisher said she might invite a friend to San Salvatore. Do you think she is telling the truth? Why do you think she said this?

7 Every visitor to San Salvatore was changed by the place. Describe the slow changes taking place in:
   (a)   Lady Caroline
   (b)   Mrs Fisher
   (c)   Mrs Arbuthnot

8 Mrs Fisher asked Mrs Arbuthnot: 'What is Mr Arbuthnot?' Why was Mrs Fisher very angry with Rose's reply?

8

1 What did Lady Caroline and Mrs Wilkins call each other?

2 What happened when Mr Wilkins had a bath?

3 What was the real reason for Mr Wilkins coming to San Salvatore?

4 Why did Mr Wilkins think Mrs Fisher was rich? Was he right?

5 Why was Mr Wilkins surprised when Mrs Fisher told him Lady Caroline was doing the housekeeping?

6 What suggestion did Mr Wilkins make about the housekeeping?

7 What did Lady Caroline offer as her present to San Salvatore?

8 Why did Mr Wilkins lead Mrs Fisher away from Lady Caroline?

9

1 Why was Mr Wilkins very pleased with Lottie?

2 Rose wrote letters to her husband. What did she do with the letters?

3 How was San Salvatore changing Mrs Fisher?

4 Rose was expecting a telegram. Why was she expecting a telegram?

5 Rose did receive a telegram. Who was it from?

6 Why did Thomas Briggs want to see Rose Arbuthnot's face again?

7 Why did Thomas Briggs ask Rose to stand in front of a painting?

8 Why did Thomas not want to see Mrs Fisher?

9 What had happened to Mrs Fisher?

10 What happened to Thomas Briggs?

10

1 Was Lady Caroline pleased with Thomas Briggs?
2 Why had Ferdinand Arundel come to visit San Salvatore?
3 Why did Lady Caroline decide to be friendly to Ferdinand Arundel?
4 Why did Rose wish her husband, Frederick, was with her?
5 But Rose did not see his look of surprise.
   (a)   Who do you think Frederick Arbuthnot and Ferdinand Arundel are?
   (b)   Why did Rose think Frederick had come to San Salvatore?

11

1 Who had Frederick Arbuthnot come to see?
2 What did Lady Caroline say when Lottie introduced her to Frederick Arbuthnot?
3 Lady Caroline looked at Thomas Briggs.
   (a)   Why had Thomas fallen in love with Lady Caroline?
   (b)   What kind of person did Lady Caroline know she was?
4 'I must stop this,' Mr Wilkins whispered to Lottie.
   (a)   What did Mr Wilkins think he must stop?
   (b)   What did Lottie do?
5 Everyone left San Salvatore on the first of May. What had happened to them all?

Glossary

1 **club** (page 7)
   Mrs Wilkins was a member of a ladies' club. She can go to a building in London and drink coffee, read the morning newspapers or have a meal. A club is not like a hotel; you have to pay to join a club.

2 **old-fashioned** (page 7)
   in an old style – not modern.

3 **Hampstead** (page 7)
   Hampstead is an area where people live in the north of London. It is an area where there are a lot of people who have plenty of money.

4 **'To Let'** (page 7)
   the owner of a castle in Italy wants visitors to live in the castle for a month, so it is the visitors who pay the owner money to live there. This money is called the rent.

5 **sighed** (page 8)
   to sigh is to breathe out making a noise. The noise shows you are sad.

6 **solicitor** (page 8)
   the business of a solicitor is to deal with wills and legal papers.

7 **allow** (page 11)
   to permit you to do something – to say you can do it.

8 **receipt** (page 11)
   a piece of paper with writing on. Someone gives you a receipt to show that you have paid money to them.

9 **expenses** (page 12)
   when the ladies are staying at the castle, they will have to give money to the cook to bring food. These are the expenses. The ladies agree they will all share the paying of these expenses.

10 **bored** (page 12)
   unhappy because you cannot find anything interesting to do.

11 **references** (page 12)
   Mrs Fisher wants the ladies to bring a paper written by a solicitor or a doctor or a banker. The paper would say that the ladies are honest. Mrs Arbuthnot says such a paper is not needed.

12 **way** – *getting her own way* (page 14)
   to get your own way is to make other people agree to do what you want.

13 **horrified** (page 15)
   very shocked and surprised about something.
14 **horse-cab** (page 17)
   a carriage pulled by one horse. The carriage takes passengers from
   one place to another like a modern taxi.
15 **winding** (page 17)
   turning and twisting.
16 **archway** (page 20)
   a piece of curved stonework going over the top of a gate.
17 **gardener** (page 20)
   a person who looks after the flowers and the plants in the garden.
18 **shutters** (page 21)
   pieces of wood which can be put over windows to keep out strong
   sunlight.
19 **enchanted** – *enchanted place* (page 21)
   a place which is so beautiful that it is magical.
20 **exclaimed** (page 25)
   to exclaim is to speak out loud in surprise.
21 **table** – *at the head of the table* (page 25)
   the person who sits at the head of the table is the most important
   person in the room. Mrs Fisher is showing the other two ladies
   that she is the most important person.
22 **poets** – *Italian of the poets* (page 26)
   one of the most famous Italian poets is Dante. Dante lived from
   1265 to 1321. The modern Italian language is very different from
   the Italian Dante wrote. If Mrs Fisher tried to speak to the
   servants in this old-fashioned Italian, they would not understand
   her very well.
23 **orchard** (page 27)
   a group of fruit trees growing together.
24 **disturbed** – *she did not want to be disturbed* (page 30)
   Lady Caroline wants to lie quietly in the garden. She does not
   want anyone to speak to her or to make a noise.
25 **terrace** (page 31)
   a flat piece of ground outside a house. A terrace is usually paved
   with stone. People can sit on chairs on a terrace or walk up and
   down.

26 **gong** (page 31)

a gong is a flat circle of metal (often brass). When the servant hits the gong with a stick, it makes a loud booming noise. This noise tells the people in the castle it is time to come for breakfast, lunch or dinner.

27 **manners** – *bad manners* (page 31)

it is good manners when you are staying with friends to come to the dining-room on time. Lady Caroline does not come to the table and so Mrs Fisher says she has bad manners.

28 **omelette** (page 32)

eggs beaten together and fried. Omelettes are made in flat circles; vegetables are put on top and then the omelette is folded in half.

29 **women** – *modern young women* (page 34)

Mrs Fisher is an old woman. She says, 'Women's heads weren't made for thinking.' and 'Pretty, young women are made to be looked at.' She learnt these things when she was young, but young women like Lady Caroline don't believe these things now. Lady Caroline wants to think and do what she wants. Mrs Fisher is annoyed, and calls her a 'modern, young woman.'

30 **selfish** (page 37)

a selfish person does not think of other people.

31 **cold** – *catch cold* (page 38)

to become ill because you are not wearing warm clothes.

32 **widow** (page 40)

a woman whose husband has died is a widow.

33 **freedom** – *enjoying her freedom* (page 42)

a married woman at the time of this story had to spend her time looking after her husband. She could not choose what she wanted to do. Mrs Wilkins had freedom at the castle because her husband was not there. She might lose that freedom when her husband arrived.

34 **furious** (page 44)

very, very angry.

35 **blossom** (page 44)

flowers which grow on trees in spring.

36 **blow up** (page 45)

to blow up is to explode with a loud bang.

37 **bills** – *housekeeping bills* (page 48)

the cook gets food from the shops, but does not pay for it. The shopkeepers write down the cost of everything she takes. These written lists are the housekeeping bills. Constanza has to pay the shopkeepers at the end of each week. If she does not pay them, she will not be able to buy more food.

38 **card** (page 52)

at the time of this story, there were rules about speaking to people. You were not supposed to speak to anyone unless you had been introduced to them. Giving a stranger your card – a piece of cardboard with your name printed on it – was a way of introducing yourself.

39 **biographies** (page 58)

a biography is a book which tells the story of a person's life.

40 **drawing-room** (page 59)

a room in a large house where people can sit together and meet visitors.

INTERMEDIATE LEVEL

Shane *by Jack Schaefer*
Old Mali and the Boy *by D. R. Sherman*
Bristol Murder *by Philip Prowse*
Tales of Goha *by Leslie Caplan*
The Smuggler *by Piers Plowright*
The Pearl *by John Steinbeck*
Things Fall Apart *by Chinua Achebe*
The Woman Who Disappeared *by Philip Prowse*
The Moon is Down *by John Steinbeck*
A Town Like Alice *by Nevil Shute*
The Queen of Death *by John Milne*
Walkabout *by James Vance Marshall*
Meet Me in Istanbul *by Richard Chisholm*
The Great Gatsby *by F. Scott Fitzgerald*
The Space Invaders *by Geoffrey Matthews*
My Cousin Rachel *by Daphne du Maurier*
I'm the King of the Castle *by Susan Hill*
Dracula *by Bram Stoker*
The Sign of Four *by Sir Arthur Conan Doyle*
The Speckled Band and Other Stories by *Sir Arthur Conan Doyle*
The Eye of the Tiger *by Wilbur Smith*
The Queen of Spades and Other Stories *by Aleksandr Pushkin*
The Diamond Hunters *by Wilbur Smith*
When Rain Clouds Gather *by Bessie Head*
Banker *by Dick Francis*
No Longer at Ease *by Chinua Achebe*
The Franchise Affair *by Josephine Tey*
The Case of the Lonely Lady *by John Milne*

For further information on the full selection of
Readers at all five levels in the series, please refer
to the Heinemann ELT Readers catalogue.

Published by Macmillan Heinemann ELT
Between Towns Road, Oxford OX4 3PP
Macmillan Heinemann ELT is an imprint of
Macmillan Publishers Limited
Companies and representatives throughout the world
Heinemann is a registered trademark of Harcourt Education, used under licence.

ISBN 978–1–4050–7291–5

This retold version by Margaret Tarner for Macmillan Readers
First published 1992
Design and illustration © Macmillan Publishers Limited 1992, 2005

This edition first published 2005

Typography by Adrian Hodgkins
Original cover template design by Jackie Hill
Cover photography by Getty

Printed in Thailand

2011 2010 2009 2008 2007
10 9 8 7 6 5 4 3